GOD'S PROMISE

BY
DIANE SARGENT

COPYRIGHTS

AUTHOR BIO

DIANE SARGENT MUCKEFUSE LOVES TO FIND THAT "JUST RIGHT BOOK", FOR STUDENTS. DIANE WAS A CLASSROOM TEACHER AND AN ELEMENTARY SCHOOL LIBRARIAN AND HAS TAUGHT MANY YEARS OF SUNDAY SCHOOL. SHE WANTED TO WRITE BOOKS TO GIVE CHILDREN A CURIOSITY FOR THE BIBLE AND HISTORY WHILE HAVING FUN READING A STORY. DIANE LOVES TO TRAVEL THE WORLD AND THE U.S. SHE LIVES IN FLORIDA AND SUMMERS IN SOUTH CAROLINA WITH HER HUSBAND JEFF.

TWO FRIENDS READY TO START THEIR SUMMER VACATION ARE THRUST BACKWARDS INTO BIBLE TIMES. JAMES IS POLISHING A ROCK HIS FATHER BROUGHT BACK FROM HIS ARCHAEOLOGY DIG IN THE MIDDLE EAST. SWOOSH, BANG JAMES AND HIS FRIEND AL ARE DRAWN INTO THE ROCK AND TUMBLE THROUGH TUNNELS AND HIT THE GROUND WITH A THUD. WHO IS THAT SCRAGGLY LOOKING MAN DRESSED IN ANIMAL SKIN?

DEDICATION

THIS BOOK IS DEDICATED TO MY AMAZING HUSBAND JEFF WHO ALWAYS ENCOURAGES ME AND MY FORMER STUDENTS OF FREEDOM ELEMENTARY WHO LISTEN TO AND READ BOOKS.

PROLOGUE

James and Al were best friends. They first met in Sunday School at First United Methodist Church in Simpsonville, South Carolina, where Al's father was the Pastor. James' father was a professor at the college in nearby Greenville where he taught Archelogy. James loved to build stuff from junk, and Al was a whiz with computers. They spent as much time together as possible. James' dad was always bringing back exciting things from his digs that he did with his students.

James and Al finished third grade and were looking forward to summer vacation.

CHAPTER 1
TREASURED ROCK

James's father was a Professor of Archeology at the college in town. He specialized in Biblical studies. James loved hearing his dad's stories when he returned from his trips around the world. The artifacts he collected filled Professor Blanchard's shelves in his study. James' Dad had just returned from the country of Jordan near the Jordan River in the Middle East.

James' favorite treasure from this dig was the shiny black stone with gold flecks that sparkled as the sun hit it.

Today James decided to look closer at the rock to see the flecks of gold up close.

Al stood behind him as he carefully reached for the stone and brought it off the shelf.

"Your Dad has so many fascinating things. Why is this your favorite?" I like it because it came from the river Jesus was baptized in.

The boys begin to take a closer look at the rock. James grabs a cloth and begins to rub the rock back and forth to get the dust off it. The stone starts to spark, and the boys are pulled swiftly and sucked into the rock.

"Ahhhhh, Yahwee!"

They spin and move swiftly through a series of tunnels.
They dump out to the ground with a thud.
"James' head is still spinning. "What just happened?"
In front of them, they see a man with long gray hair and a
scraggly beard wearing a tattered robe.
Al, "Where are we, and who is that old guy that looks like
Noah from the Bible?"

CHAPTER 2
WHERE ARE WE?

Standing in front of them is a massive tree with powerful thick branches that reach out like monster arms. Powerful hammering noises and people shouting orders echo through the trees. James and Al climb high up to gain a better view of what is going on. The scraggly, hairy man wearing the animal skin robe is studying a strange-looking scroll and measuring wood with a string. To the left, they see an enormous structure as tall as a five-story building that looks like the underside of a boat. They hear many people speaking below the tree, "Noah must be crazy or drunk. Why would he waste time building a boat when no water is nearby?"

Al looks at James with a puzzled look. His friend looked like a caveman dressed in animal skins that hung like a dress. James noticed a cool breeze under his clothing made of some animal skin that he was wearing. Could we truly be back in Noah's time? How did this happen?

Al knows what James is thinking. "I know this all seems so insane." James responds, "We were in my bedroom looking at the rock just minutes ago." James can feel the rock in his hand.

CHAPTER 3
MEETING NOAH

The last thing we were doing was polishing your dad's rock. Then we are here with Noah! I wonder what Mrs. Smith would say if she could see us? Last week she talked about Noah and the Ark in our Sunday School Class.

"Can you remember the details of the story Al?" "Hmm", Al scrunches up his face, pokes the middle of his glasses and closes his eyes. After a few moments, his face lights up, and he starts to tell the story of Noah and the Ark. "God provided Noah with exact dimensions and what materials to use. God told him to collect creatures from all over and be ready to take them aboard. Hey, you know what? I have a Bible App on my phone that is in my pocket. Let's look up the Noah story." Al opens up his phone. "That's weird; the only app on my phone is the Bible App. Genesis is the first book in the Bible. It starts in Genesis, Chapter 6."

"God was not happy with the humans in the world, and he was ready to wipe them out!"

Just as Al was reading the story in his app, Noah appeared. "Hey, boys, we need help. Would you like to help? I can't pay you, but I could give you food and a place to rest your head." We looked at each other, shrugged our shoulders, and both said at the same time as one voice. "Sure."

CHAPTER 4
GAINING NOAH'S TRUST

Noah is looking at us with a suspicious expression. "Whose kin are you?" Al had to think fast on that one. "We are your kin from the valley." "I remember your sons came to see our cousins in our village last year to trade goods," replied Al. "Oh, very good you may not think I am a fool like everyone else around here. God told me he was disappointed in mankind and the evil and violence that fills the world. God is going to wipe out these people. God is pleased with me and has instructed me to build an Ark and bring my family and creatures."

James tells Noah, "We believe you; we know God communicates with you. How could we possibly think what God says is foolish." "It is great that you are kin, and when the floods come, you will be safe with us on the boat.

I need all the help I can get today lifting and hammering timbers."

"Shem, Ham, I have some help for you." Noah shouts towards them. Shem and Ham looked at us with a cautious look. We hear them whispering to each other, "Who are these boys and where did they come from?" "Shem, we need all the help we can get so let's not worry about who and where they came from."

Shem and Al grabbed one side of the timber, and James and Ham got the other. Ham brought out a lever to help get the frame started. The wood began to move into position. Snap! The lever popped, and the timber was rolling right at Noah! Noah yelled, "Run!"

CHAPTER 5
CLOSE CALL

"That was close. Too close, Father. We need to forget about making this huge ship," Shem declared.

"No, this is God's command to me, sons. I have to do what he asks. The Ark will be my family's survival when the floods come."

Al and I had to come up with a plan to help with this humongous task.

"Al, let's look at your app and see if we can brainstorm a better way to help with these huge logs."

After looking at Noah's story in the app and reading the information, Al came up with a unique but tremendous idea!

"Ham, Shem, come here. I think I know how we can make this job easier on all of us."

Ham questions, "Al, you are but a boy; what could you know about building a boat?"

Shem questions, "Where did you come from? Do we know your family? Your tribe?"

"I come from a village east of the valley below."

"Ham, "It won't hurt to listen to him. This entire job is nothing but an ongoing   nightmare." Shem says.

Al sat down with them and began to draw his plan with a stick in the sand.

CHAPTER 6
AL HAS A PLAN

When they looked at what Al was drawing, they were surprised to see an elephant drawn in the sand.

"We can use the elephant's strength to pull the heavy timbers. Tie the rope around the elephant's neck and tie the other end to the timber." Shem leads the Elephant to where the timber must go. Amazingly the Elephant sensed what they needed and obeyed every command. By the end of the day, all the heavy logs were in place. We reviewed the plans and the directions that God gave Noah.

"So. make yourself an ark of Cyprus Wood, make rooms in it, and coat it with pitch inside and out. The ark is three hundred cubits long, fifty cubits wide, and thirty cubits high. Make a roof for it, leaving an opening one cubit high below the roof. Put a door in the side of the ark and make lower, middle, and upper decks."

James has a questioning look. How big is a cubit? Can you look that up, Al?

It is based on measuring a man's arm from his elbow to the end of his middle finger, about 18 inches.

We all sat and rested at the end of the day; the bottom of the ark was complete. Noah's wife and daughters made us a feast of meats, fruit, and loaves of bread that we all devoured like lions.

Shem and Ham began to discuss and look over a scroll of the plans of the ark. The ship would have to contain storage for food, animals, and people. Each deck would have rooms separating animals and quarters for the family to stay in. "It reminds me of the cruise ship I went on with my Grandma last year. Can we have a surf pool?" James giggles.

CHAPTER 7
GET TO WORK

Al and James are lying in the tent, talking about the day and what they think will happen in the future. Al said with a shaky voice, "I miss being at home and mom's cooking. I even miss my sister." Do you think our families have figured out where we are?

James, I wondered that too. We are here for a reason. We are seeing God's hands at work. Let's pray about it and see what God tells us.

In the morning, the boys awoke to what sounded like elephants trumpeting in the distance. When they left the tent to investigate, they saw a crowd of animals of every kind, like the zoo, had opened its gates. The animals were running wild! Noah, with sons Shem, Ham, and Japheth, were huddled around the sand looking at a drawing. Al figured they were planning what would go on each deck. He glanced at his phone app and reviewed what should go on the first floor. He crouched down and drew a square in the sand for each room. On floor one, there would be spaces for each kind of bird. The brothers were constructing a family living quarters adding bedding and gathering areas. Deck two held many store rooms for grains, straws, dried meat, and various supplies for humans and beasts. Deck Three had two cisterns to collect additional water. We would have to build many rooms to accommodate each species of animal. Noah and his sons stared with open mouths at Al. "You are a genius! How did you come up with such detail?" "Ahh, just something I dreamed up in my sleep."

CHAPTER 8
ANIMAL MADNESS

The sunlight streamed in through the gaping tent flaps. "Caaa, Caaa. Weeep Weeep, Awwwap," the sounds woke Al and James. Al rubbed the sleep from his eyes and peeked outside. "What is going on? It sounds like a bird sanctuary out there!" James got up from his mat. They heard a thunderous sound of hooves running past the tent. James stepped barefoot out of the tent to see what was happening. Squish went his toes. "Ahh, yuck!" He looked down at his foot even though he could already smell that his foot was in a giant pile of poop! He tried not to vomit, but the smell was just too much. There were giraffes, pandas, lions, alligators, parrots, and animals of every species and size. "I don't know why we are so shocked; this is Noah's story. We know what happens. We better get started. Let's see what Noah needs from us today."

Noah, his sons, and grandsons were gathered around the fire, talking about what their next steps would be.

"Now that the animals are arriving, we must prepare for them. James and Ham, you lay down the bedding in the stalls. Japheth and Al make sure the stalls have water and food for each animal.", Noah directed.

God commanded, "You are to take every kind of food for your family and the animals."

"Our job today is to cut local grass and grains for the animals and bring them into the storerooms. Let's get to it, Al." James shouted out orders as if he was in charge.

Noah saw the boys hot and sweaty from their work in the fields. "Boys, come here and take some time to rest."

Noah gives them each a cup of water and a hunk of bread. "You have worked hard and filled the grain storage with barley and wheat today. Would it be possible for you to help the ladies grind grain into flour?" James responds, "Yes, we would happily help grind flour."

Noah's tired voice states, "We are in a hurry since the animals have started to come. The rain will be here soon too."

James says, "Noah, we have been watching the animals today, and we are amazed at how the animals get along. We saw a lion sitting by a gazelle. I thought they ate gazelles. We saw a coyote walk right by a chicken. Noah shook his head and beard." "I know it must be God's hand. I can't understand why the prey sits with the attacker."

CHAPTER 9
TIME IS RUNNING OUT

The crowds of villagers are getting larger and louder every day. In mocking tones they shout "Noah, you are going to need those elephants to pull that boat to the ocean. Do you think they can carry it for hundreds of miles?" Laughter from the crowd. "Surely Noah has gone crazy to build a ship so large when we have no water here. He hears voices from God! Ha, telling him what to do!"
Continued laughter.
James and Al are busy from sunup to sundown gathering food for animals and Noah's family to fill up the Ark. Shem and Ham are emptying the storage from the tents to the ship. As James walks down the gangplank, he gets a nudge and jumps back to find his elephant friend poking at him. His friends will never believe what he has witnessed. Shem and Japheth are now at the ship's door recording the animals they are loading on the Ark today. On a stone tablet, not a digital tablet. Seven pairs of animals they consider clean by their religion to eat. One pair of unclean animals. Sons Shem and Ham showed the boys what stalls held what animals so that they could help with the loading. When the kangaroos came bouncing in, Al couldn't help but squeal. When they were in front of him, he saw a baby joey lift his head out of his mama's pouch. We continued to help the animals on the Ark the entire day. James jumps on the back of an Ostrich and corals it onto the boat. The smells and loud sounds of all the creatures surrounded them. The last ones on board for the night were the hippos. James questions, "Will this Ark hold the weight of all these creatures?" Al replies, "We followed God's plans, so we know it will be strong enough and a safe place for all of us."

CHAPTER 10
ANIMALS GROUPING UP

A large group of fuzzy black and white Pandas is coming in. "Did you know the group of pandas is called a cupboard of pandas." "How do you know that" James questions. " It's here on the app. What each group of animals is called." Al responds with a giggle.
"Let me see that!" James yanks the phone out of Al's hands.
"Here comes a group of flamingos. Let's see what they are. A flamboyance of flamingos." "I see a bunch of baboons headed this way. They are called a congress of baboons." The animals continued to come for days and days. We helped to move them into the Ark.
The Villagers were watching as all these animals arrived. They continued to shout at Noah that he was crazy and should be feasting on these animals.
The heavy rains started as the last batch of animals arrived.

CHAPTER 11
THE FLOOD

The rain was coming down the side of the Ark like a rushing waterfall. It was time to close up the plank and doors. Noah called for his sons and all his kin to get on board. He looked out at the people from his village, and tears streamed down his face. These were his neighbors. Noah knew none of the villagers would survive. Some of the people were still mocking him.

James knew from his reading the book of Genesis in the Bible that the rain would last for forty days and forty nights.

The days were dark and long. They could watch from the port holes and on deck when it was safe. Soon the tops of the trees became covered over with waves. Thrashing through the white cap waves were people, trees, and creatures bouncing around like toys in the water. The mountains soon began to disappear under the billowing waves. Noah felt great sadness and prayed a lot of the time. Noah was faithful and knew God had a plan.

James and Al were extremely busy keeping the animals fed and happy. Tiny, their elephant friend, even learned some tricks thanks to James. He could stand on his back legs while giving a high five with his front leg.

Al often brought baby animals into their cabin to sleep with at night. James became used to waking up to tiger cubs chewing on his blanket or a baby kangaroo hopping from bunk to bunk.

CHAPTER 12
IS IT SAFE?

Many, many days went by with rain and more rain. This morning they all woke up to silence: no pounding rain, no big waves slapping the boat.

"James, do you hear that?" "No, what?" questions Al. "That's it; there is no rain hitting the deck." Al ran to look out a porthole. "You are right. I don't see a speck of rain." "Noah, the rain has stopped. We can go out!"

Noah spoke in a calming voice, "It is too dangerous just to open the door and venture out. We need to know there is land to put our feet on. Be patient."

Patient they would have to be. One hundred and fifty days later. Noah sent out a bird to see what would happen. It quickly returned for it had no dry land to set on. He would try this two more times before he declared it a success. The dove came back with an olive branch in her beak.

The door was not easy to open, but after pushing and prying, they were able to drop it open.

Al ran to Tiny the elephant and let her and the other elephants out first. They bellowed a happy troooo on the way out. Noah assigned jobs to all his family including Al and James.

James began with the birds; they happily flapped their wings on the way out of the Ark.

EEEEEe could be heard as the primates jumped and swung from the rafters. It was better than visiting any zoo and watching all these happy animals leave the ship.

CHAPTER 13
GOD'S PROMISE

A brilliant rainbow was beaming down on the Ark and the land. Noah, his wife, sons, daughters, Al, and James looked upward with a beaming smiles and happy hearts. They had endured a long and challenging time on the sea, but now they were safe. God sent the rainbow as a promise that he would not destroy the earth with a flood again. "James, I will never look at a rainbow again without remembering this journey." "Al, I don't know why we were sent here, but I will never forget this time and the experience of being with Noah." "James, the sad part is, who can we tell about this experience? No one would believe us." "Al, it might make a great bedtime story to tell our children someday." Both Al and James said at the same time, "It is time to go home."

James and Al retrieved the rock from their bunk in the Ark. They went to Noah to say goodbye and thank you. Noah said, "Where will you go? There is no one left but us?"

Al, "We are traveling back to another time." Noah hugged the boys and watched them walk off. Al and James sat down rubbed the stone, and were drawn back into the stone as a vapor.

CHAPTER 14
HOME AT LAST

"James, it is dinner time! Is Al staying to eat with us?" The boys stepped into the kitchen, and James's mom could smell the aroma of thousands of animals. "Where have you been? You smell like the zoo." James replied, "that's where we came from; we went to the city zoo for the day."

GLOSSARY

Archaeology -the scientific study of material remains (such as tools, pottery, jewelry, stone walls, and monuments) of past human life and activities.

Artifact- An artifact is an object made by a human being. Artifacts include art, tools, and clothing made by people of any time and place. The term can also be used to refer to the remains of an object, such as a shard of broken pottery or glassware.

Kin — another word for family members

Cistern - A cistern is an underground tank that holds water. A long time ago, cistern water was used for drinking.

FUN FACTS

The Ark was the same size as 250 railroad cars.
Noah became a father at 500 years old.
Noah's grandfather Methuselah, lived until he was 969 years old.
Noah lived to be 950 years old.
The Ark construction would have taken approximately 100 years.
The Ark was built to be three stories high with many compartments in it.
The Ark was said to have landed on Mount Ararat in Turkey. No one knows for sure if any part of the Ark is still around. There have been many theories and sightings of things they thought were the Ark but no factual knowledge of where it went to.

BIBLIOGRAPHY FOR NOAH

https://www.thefactsite.com/noahs-ark-facts/ # Fact Site, Krehbiel Andrew, 32 Interesting Things about Noah and his Ark, December 12, 2022.

Merriamwebster.com 2023

Vocabulary.com 2023

Education.Nationalgeographic.org, Resource Encyclopedia

https://www.biblica.com/ Bouchard Karen, 7 Things you Might Not Know about Noah's Ark. March 22, 2019.

Mysteries of the Bible, the Enduring Questions of the Scriptures. Reader's Digest Association, 1988

Quest Study Bible NIV

The Sun.com. What is a group of Pandas called? Boroff David May 21, 202158 ET, May 21 2

Reader's Digest, Spektor Brandon, 27 Hilarious (but totally real) Names of Animals. July 27,2021.1

https://www.thefactsite.com/noahs-ark-facts/

www.ingramcontent.com/pod-product-compliance
Lightning Source LLC
Chambersburg PA
CBHW041030170626

46815CB00001B/41